Precious Water

A Book of Thanks

Brigitte Weninger

Anne Möller

Look at this glass of water.

It is so clear that you can see right through it.

The little drops of water on the glass glitter like jewels, and they are just as precious.

All living things need water.

Without water, the plants would die.

Without water, the animals would die.

Without water, people would die.

The whole world would be dead
if there were no water.

But luckily, we do have water: water that falls from the sky, water in the rivers and lakes and deep beneath the ground.

Ice and snow are frozen water.

And the seas are made of salt water.

I give my plants a little water so they won't wilt.

I give my cat a little water
so she won't be thirsty.

And I drink some water too.
How good it tastes!

I hope we will always have enough water for
the plants and animals and people on earth.
I am so thankful for this precious water.

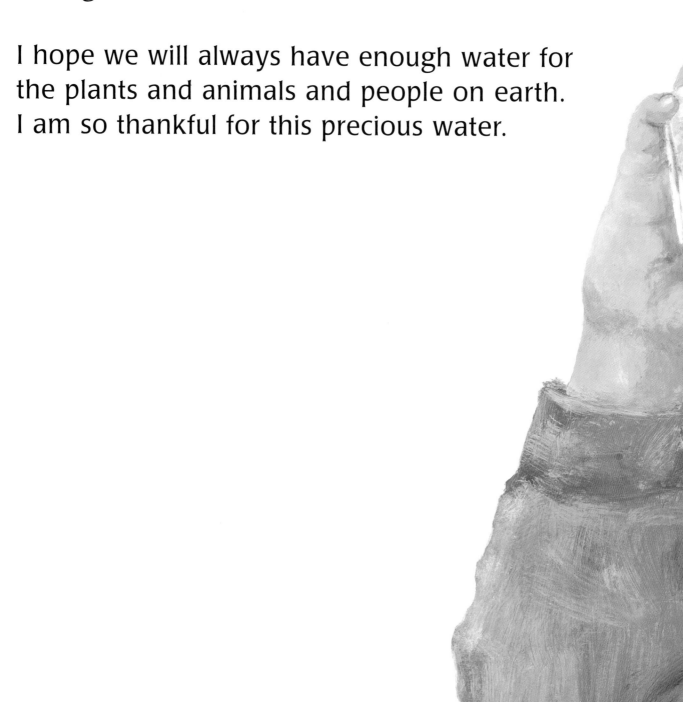